Standing Guard

And other Short Stories

Roy Bolland

Author of 'The Battle for the Kingdoms'
Abridged excerpt included at back of book

This edition first published by Amazon

Copyright: © 2023 Roy Bolland

Roy Bolland has asserted the right to be identified as

the author of this work in accordance with the

Copyright, Designs and Patents act 1988

ISBN: 9798567982051

With thanks to Marjorie for passing on her knowledge
and both Marjorie and Ramon for their friendship.

Also thanks to my son Nathan who has been a great help
in compiling this book and I am more than
thankful for his contribution.

Contents

Standing Guard

He had heard the sound on and off over the last few years and this was the third time in as many days. He had heard it again; and louder this time and clearer. It was a child's voice of that he was quite certain and it had ended with a plaintive cry for help.

He awoke from his not unusual Sunday afternoon nap startled by the noise, and rushed upstairs to the small bedroom at the rear of the house from which seemed to be from where the sound had emanated. Neither sight nor sound met him as he pushed open wide the door, and standing, breathing heavily after his upward dash from the lounge, he collected his senses and closed his eyes tight shut and listened...nothing; just pure, clear, forever seemingly ongoing silence, which after a short period of time was broken only by his own sharp intake of breath.

He slowly sat down on the small bed that as small as it was still took up more than half of the room, and with his elbows upon his knees, his head cradled in his upturned hands, he let his thoughts wander. His heart became heavy as he remembered that it had been five years almost to the day since the laughter had suddenly, with little warning, made exit from his life.

He had, shortly after that terrible time thought seriously of leaving the area and the past and all its consequences behind, and yet even as he had made his mind up to go, he knew he wouldn't. After just a matter of months his wife, the mother of his child had packed and left. He hadn't blamed her; not for anything, but she'd said that it was too painful for her now and she knew that while she remained it would never go away. She went alone of course. He had to stay.

He sat straighter and relaxed his hands upon his lap, lifted his head and slowly looked around the room. His eyes moved, somewhat warily, to view the back of the now closed door and the short dressing gown that still hung there on its peg and to the right of that, another peg upon which were hung by their long laces, the smallest pair of football boots he had ever seen. They had in comparison appeared big when he had brought them home and placed them on the floor next to Simon's feet; he was four then but had even seemed younger than that.

He'd had a heart operation when he was merely six months old, quite a major one, but he had struggled remarkably to survive it, and on the so few occasions when he had let all the frustration and pain show, he knew his dad would be there. Except for his size no-one would have been any the wiser that there had ever been a problem at all. The lad never gave in to anything. He had started pre-school and after lessons -which weren't really lessons but just a way of meeting and making friends- tried his hand at all the sports with the other kids on the village field.

He'd intended even at that early age; 'I'm going to be a footballer dad and better than Beckham,' he'd shouted gleefully as he'd returned home after scoring at least once. He had to be careful that he didn't overdo it but he wanted to be as normal a lad as he could. He'd asked for, and got, a cowboy outfit from Father Christmas, how could he refuse, and he wouldn't take it off till New Year.

He turned his head to the right and his eyes lit up as he surveyed 'Simon's Gallery.' Those were the words -written surprisingly well for a five year old in boldly written blue letters on white card above the selection of drawings, some from school and some drawn or painted in this very same room, Tiger, the cat, a stray that had lived with them for some time until it presumably had found more attentive accommodation elsewhere, was pictured in a scene between the goal-posts saving the ball from entering the net. 'It can't have been a shot of yours Simon,' he'd said at the time- in fact he recalled that he had said it every time on seeing the purple cat with its green face, and it's yellow paws clutching the ball- 'he wouldn't have saved one of yours.' 'We are the champions,' Simon would sing and they had both fallen about on the bed laughing and pretending to fight.

He rose from his seated position on that now silent and seemingly fragile bed and walked the few steps to the wardrobe. After some discussion Simon had got his way and had painted it in the colours of his school team. 'I'll do it,' he'd said, and so, after ensuring for his mother's sake more than his own, that the carpet and furniture were well protected, he'd left him to it. He opened the single door and peered within, his eyes straining to see the contents. He hadn't looked inside for some time and somehow felt like an intruder, out of time, searching for sacred relics. His eyes wandered slowly from the sight of the school blazers and the grey trousers, and then to the football kit all hanging neatly on hangers and his well worn cowboy outfit protected by polythene covering... waiting it seemed. Three pairs of shoes and a hardly worn pair of football boots reclined in the shadow in the corner, also it seemed, waiting. He remembered his son standing, guns at the ready with his cowboy hat, waistcoat and chaps, there was no sheriff tougher; guarding his brand new football strip hanging just inside the wardrobe door, 'Look at me dad, no-one will get past me'

He closed the wardrobe door quietly and slowly and made his way across to the little desk by the window.

Another, this time smaller, collection of pictures-if by the slightest chance of ill luck he couldn't for some unaccountable reason be a footballer, or a sheriff, he was going to be an artist, what plans this little boy had, 'but I won't cut my ear off dad,' he'd said, trying not to alarm his father. Now there were pictures of mum and dad. At work and at play, yellow, purple and pink and surprising him yet again how each of them must have looked through Simon's eyes. He wished he'd have been half as agile as the drawings made him appear, in one picture he was playing football with his son and his foot was kicking over the back of his own head and his knee was jointed the opposite way. He smiled a rare smile at that.

And there was a picture of mum with an arrow pointing to her swollen tummy and the words in Simon's best handwriting, Julies in here. A lump came into his throat and his eyes moistened and he turned his head away and looked out of the window to the garden and the field beyond. The field where kids were still playing even though it was now well past tea-time; it was cricket now; it was the season for it. Reflected in the window pane, the room behind him looked still, and in the half light increasingly empty and lonely.

He closed the door quietly behind him and descended the stairs and walked softly into the lounge and regained his seat from where he had so recently been awakened it seemed by the sound of crying. Simon's mum had lost the baby, and within six months Simon's heart had given up its fight for survival, he had struggled valiantly yet again and his dad was there to comfort him, especially on those few occasions when he had cried. The hospital had sent him home, there was nothing more they could do and he'd wanted to be at home with all his things. He had of course known he was ill but hadn't known how ill he really was. He had passed away quietly in that very same bed in that small bedroom upstairs... He had to stay.

Until Proven Guilty

Tramping down the highway of broken dreams my mind became assailed by that which stole from a dark and wearisome corner and slowly but most certainly burrowed its way into my unconscious. Memories of my not too-distant past; dead and trying to be buried, awakened me begrudgingly from my nether world of imaginings. Turning my head ever so slowly from one side to the other and staring through blinking eyes with no sense yet of being aware of whether I was alive or dead or just plain indifferent to my surroundings, I became conscious of the knowledge that I was not alone.

Beside me in this quagmire of tossed and twisted sheets was Icaron. She who from another world of aeons ago, before the rumble had become a roar and while the wind was yet just a whisper had brought me back from the brink and had not saved me, but had set me firmly down in this dungeon of despair which was now my only home, she had weaved her spell so well that I had become as a collapsed puppet just waiting for her pull of the strings to make me active and to do her bidding.

This Thusean female with the pure white face and limpid yellow eyes pulled the bedclothes back across her naked form and then realising that she been brought to consciousness not by her own endeavours but by the writhing of the poltroon by her side, snapped her eyes wide open as a snake might at its first sight of its intended victim.

Her hooded eyes fixed on me, "Paulus you have betrayed my rest once again and you know how much I require my forays into the unknown where my desires are met with the dark forces that seduce me so delectably."

I shrank from her in fear and loathing and did no more than offer my cringing apologies. "Icaron my love and my protector save me from the fires that burn within me as you once did so many years ago."

She smiled her almost impossibly beautiful smile and curling herself up in a tight ball murmured to me, "There will be time enough for that when the night is upon us yet again," and she slept the rest of the morning through.

The Thuseans had conquered Earth, before even my imaginings had made me aware of their existence. It had been they who had brought me to this, by way of the deep and still unburied memory. I had tried my best to tell them my story but all my outpourings would not satisfy their craving for knowledge of me. Then they had taken upon themselves the form of Earthmen such as I myself was, in an attempt to draw from me more than my shattered senses could divulge.

I did not hear the key in the lock but the sound of the bolts sliding back on the door with the snap of metal released from its restraint woke me from my preoccupation. "Here take it and eat," snapped the white coated Thusean in his Earthly guise and he pushed the amply filled plate along the table toward me. "No more?" I questioned feebly. "No more," he retorted and slammed the door shut behind him and drew the bolts back into place. There was never enough for both Icaron and I.

I woke her gently, and upon seeing the food before her she rose from the bed still naked and commenced to take her share, then returning once more to the bed she sat upright with her back to the wall and began to eat. After a while she proffered the same question as always, "No more?" and I responded with the same answer that I had been given by the one who had brought it.

She shrugged her shoulders resignedly and set about to consume her sparse share. Almost as soon as we had finished that brief repast, the door opened again to allow in the bearer of the liquid refreshment. How did they know? Could these Thuseans see through walls and observe us as if they were here in this very place? It seemed that as slow or as quickly as we had eaten of the meal, they were at our side with the liquid; not too soon and not too late. This was not the one who had brought the food but another, smaller man with a high furrowed brow who gave the impression of being somewhat more articulate than the other. Even so he said little, and spoke only to me. "Did you eat well; was everything to your satisfaction?"

I had said so many times on so many different occasions that the food even though hardly palatable was not near enough, and weary with the thought of repeating myself yet again, I said nothing. The liquid was in a large plastic beaker, and was a mixture of water and other ingredients of which I knew not what. What I did know was that Icaron and I would sleep for a few hours after the imbibing of it.

"I will return later after you have rested and then you will accompany me and you will speak again with my superior, this time at some length," he said, and he too left the room and locked the door behind him. We drank the cool and pleasant tasting brew from the one container and drifted slowly into unconsciousness whilst I dreamt of countless corridors and even more doors.

Some short time after we had reawakened the noise of footsteps sounded outside, and the door was opened yet again. This time there were three of them. Still relaxed after my period of rest, I offered no resistance as the Thuseans strapped me in a jacket and frogmarched me down the passage; to the right and then to the left and down a long flight of stairs and through one door and another until we arrived at our destination.

Another Thusean with a thick shock of unruly red hair and a sallow complexion sat behind a large desk with an open file in front of him. He raised his head, motioned me to sit and dismissed those who had brought me here. "Do not venture but further than the outside of the door," he instructed them and they nodded in unison and made their exit.

He glanced at the file again for what seemed an interminable amount of time and yet was probably just minutes. "Paulus," he addressed me, "can you not understand that we are trying to be as helpful as we can to attempt to make your stay here rewarding, for your sake as much as for our own?" then taking note of my annoyance at the binding surrounding me, "are you comfortable; would you like me to release you from that cumbersome vestment?"

"It might be less painful," I answered and he released me from my fastening.

"That may be more relaxing for you, yes?

Questions, questions and more questions, there appeared not one who could give me any answers. Many times I had been before this Thusean or another and yet it was always the same. Hardly a word escaped their mouth that was not a question.

He drew himself closer across the desk and with a softening of the eye asked me, "Why did you kill your pregnant wife Paulus, was it because she had a lover?" My head would explode if I ever heard that question again. "You had found out had you not, that someone was seeing your wife behind your back and that the unborn baby may not have been yours. Am I correct?" He regained his seat.

I ran my free hands over my scalp and pulled and tugged at my hair in despair, screaming at the top of my voice. "Why do you not believe me? I have told you a thousand times that I came upon the Thusean molesting my wife." I was breathing heavily now and felt that my brain was about to burst. "He fought me off and then he produced a knife and stabbed at both of us and…" I broke down in tears now and in my anger and frustration beat down upon the desktop. …"I wrested the knife from his grip and turned it upon him but not before he had stabbed repeatedly at my wife and the unborn life that was within her. I am innocent I tell you, I am not a murderer, do you think I would kill my wife and destroy the birth of my own flesh and blood?"

"There was only one body Paulus," he interjected, "not counting the dead unborn child."

"I must have merely injured her attacker," I began again, "for when I had turned from my attempts to resuscitate her he had gone, as if spirited away into thin air."

"That was very convenient for you was it not Paulus? These Thuseans must be magicians… or Wizards perhaps to spirit themselves away. What exactly do these people look like, are they…?"

"They are like you," I screamed banging again on the desktop.

"Then they are like you too Paulus, the very same are they not; just as you or I. Human beings from this same planet Earth, not from somewhere else in this universe." His voice softened as he uttered those last words, but I was in no mood for sympathy I jumped up from my chair, tugged again at my hair, then banged with both hands on the desk yet again and screamed and yelled at him that he was covering up for one of his own. He reached his hand quickly to the side of his desk and the door burst open and the three who had brought me there caught hold of me and restrained me once more in the jacket, while my legs kicked out at them.

The interrogator shouted above the noise of my struggling. "We know every word you say Paulus, we know the truth and you will eventually tell us from your own lips and then we will have an end to all this. Take him back to his room gentlemen." And he turned and left the room by another door.

How did, they know, I wondered as I lay on my bed after the ordeal? How could, they know? The same way in which they knew when we had arisen, when we were ready to eat and then when we were ready to drink. But there was just Icaron and I, and *I* did not reveal this information to them. Then like a light being switched on in my brain I knew that it was she. The Thusean who had once saved me had now revealed all my secrets to her own kind. She had betrayed me.

She lay beside me now deep in slumber, her naked body curled up as before. How could she sleep, so like an innocent child, did she not carry any guilt for what she had done? I reached over to her and kissed her softly on her lips. She murmured and turned toward me, I caressed her body gently and reached my fingers around her throat… and squeezed.

She gasped for breath as she slowly became aware of what was happening and she clawed at me and tried to scratch out my eyes. As the pain hit me I relaxed my grip and she pushed me onto the floor and sprang on top of me, kicking and punching and with her nails and teeth ripped into my flesh.

I twisted away and regained the upper hand and drove my fist into her face time and again until my knuckles were bleeding, I lifted her head and banged it repeatedly on the cold bare floor. A pool of blood slowly oozed from behind her ear and spread out on the floor framing her white face. Her body slumped and lay limp and lifeless. She would betray me no more.

The sound of people running down the corridor caused me to look to the door as I sat dejectedly with my back against the wall. The bolts slid back; I was glad that they were here. They ignored Icaron and I did not care. I was defeated I had no concern for her or anyone. I felt the touch of the needle as it entered my arm and that same sweet relief that usually came from the contents of the plastic beaker overtook my senses and I slept.

I opened my eyes and the piercing of a bright light caused me to close them again. I opened them, this time slowly, and realised that it was a light such as that that I had in my own room which was perpetually on except when rest time came and it was dimmed. This light must have been twenty feet above me and well out of my reach. I was lying on a floor covering of soft padding, so deep that as I pushed my hand into it I could feel no solid part beneath me. I came more clearly to my senses and looked cautiously around me. The walls up to the ceiling were of the same material. I had been here only once before when they had dragged me kicking and screaming from the place where my wife had been butchered. I lay down again and yielded once more to the call of Morpheus.

It was some days before I was returned to my room where everything had been scrupulously cleaned, and no doubt searched in my absence. I was given food to eat and as before, without being called for, the Thusean with the furrowed brow and the sympathetic eyes brought in the liquid refreshment. Later the light but dimmed and I knew it was time for rest. I slid between the sheets and fell asleep. It was later in the night that I was awakened by a kiss on my lips by the naked smiling Icaron, as her yellow eyes sought me out, her white face stark in the half light. Then…inside the endless cavernous places of my mind, appearing from within the very soul of me and echoing on and on and on until I felt my brain was bleeding; came an ascending silent scream which only Icaron heard.

As was usual on occasions such as this, the surveillance system in the light upon the ceiling that was an essential part in every secure unit in the asylum, recorded nothing.

Going Straight

The bell above the door tinkled to announce his arrival, almost everyone looked up and gave the new customer a fleeting glance, but even that could be too much, as he had known previously to his cost. Too much attention he could do without, still he was dressed for the occasion, with the Times newspaper stuck under his arm.

The café, in this holiday resort town was a cut above the rest, with perhaps a dozen blends of coffee and a variety of herbal, Indian and China teas and a menu bursting with a variety of snacks, the place was a haven for tourists away from the madness on the streets; carnival week was always the busiest.

He lived locally and called here perhaps half a dozen times a year.

Ordering and paying for a large Mocha he seated himself at a table for two, with a good view of the door and the coat rack in the corner.

Wearing a new pair of slacks and a summer shirt; not too ostentatious just enough to show the casual observer that he wasn't a complete stranger to money, and he added to this image by spreading the financial section of the newspaper on the table in front of him. It may as well have been printed in Chinese, for he understood not one jot. The only thing he knew about money was what he had in his pocket. After a while he looked at his watch as if expecting someone; appearance was everything.

Five minutes elapsed and the doorbell sounded again, this time admitting a party of four people of pensionable age.

"What a scorcher," said one of the women to the counter assistant, "Yeah," she replied, giving the distinct impression that she would rather be anywhere else than where she was. No change there then she thought as she turned back to the company where a small argument was going on between the two men, both short and balding, coats over their arms, and perspiring madly.

"Listen Stan you got the coffees earlier, I'll get these and you can buy a couple of drinks later, if that'll make you happy."

"OK" said Stan reluctantly.

They stood at the counter viewing the menu. "We'll have four cappuccinos" Bill said ordering for everyone, and turning to the others, "Shall we have a light snack?" "Ooh please!" said the ladies replying as one.

They decided on four creamy scones and some Bara Brith. Bill ferreted in his coat pocket for his wallet, relieved it of what looked like two crisp twenty pound notes, and replaced his wallet in his inside coat pocket.

Laughing and talking, they made their way to the table by the window, at the far end of the room overlooking the garden area.

Bill's wife Sarah collected the coats and hung them on the rack, and tugging on her bra strap at the shoulder attempting to readjust herself in an effort to cool down, made her way back to join the excited conversation at the table, where Bill and Stan were again arguing about who should have paid.

A few minutes later after noting that people were more intent on watching the antics of the frolicsome four, he looked at his watch again, emitted a deep sigh, rolled his newspaper up, stood up and draining his coffee cup quietly easing back his chair, he strolled across to the coat rack, took Bill's coat off its peg and draping it over his arm, walked nonchalantly out of the café and into the hustle and bustle of the busy street.

Once outside in the street, he crossed over to the other side and into the department store, where he located the customer toilets. Inside the cubicle he quickly emptied the pockets of the stolen coat. Not a bad haul he thought as he opened the wallet, inside were ten or twelve twenty pound notes, two tenners and a fiver, (his instincts had been right, our Bill, had just had a pay out from the hole in the wall). After glancing at the credit cards he put them back in the wallet; leave the old chap something he thought, they were too much hassle anyway. In the outer pockets he found a gold wrist watch and about seven pounds in change.

Pocketing his ill-gotten gains, he hung the coat on the hook on the back of the cubicle door, flushed the toilet, opened the door fully, and seeing no body about, washed his hands, straightened his hair in the mirror and exited the gents, then the store. He jumped on a bus that was just about to leave the stop and travelled contentedly to the top end of town.

He was known as Judd, his given name being George, and he had moved to this area with his parents when he was a kid of perhaps four or five. Seven years later his father upped and left, and Judd was left with his mother in a shabby flat where he lived for the next five years, with her and a succession of "uncles" of every colour and persuasion.

As soon as he was old enough, he was doing odd jobs for the local hoodlums, for cash which filled his pockets and fuelled his lifestyle. He wasn't that bad a lad really, but being the way he'd been brought up with no decent role models, he had been influenced by the wrong sort and gone for the easy money. Still, it was better than working, if you could find a job that was.

Three stops later he jumped off the bus, and two streets of old Victorian houses on the left and the next right and he was home.

He'd lived at the top flat here for the last six years. He put the key in the door and in he went, "Hello doll," he called as he closed the door behind him. "Hi Judd," replied Yvonne from the kitchen. "I'm just making a drink would you like one?" "No thanks I've just had one," he said as he entered the room. She kissed him warmly on the lips, "What have you been up to sweetheart?" then noticing him fingering the gold watch, "Not again Judd, please, not again." "It was too easy Yvonne, a small group of pensioners, holidaymakers, that's all, they won't miss it."

She burst into tears, pensioners, pensioners, she screamed at him, what are next, babies and people in wheelchairs?" "Don't you realise that's probably all they've got, it's more than likely taken them all year to save up for a holiday down here, you know how expensive it is, especially in carnival week." "And I thought you'd changed Judd. I was talking to Dad earlier on the phone, and he said he could get you a job down home with him at the auction rooms." "I bet the money's not a lot," he interrupted with a feeble stab at humour which didn't go down well at all. Bursting into tears again, she said, "With the qualifications I've got now from training college I could easily get a job down home, they're crying out for nurses, and now you've spoilt it all."

"Take it back, take it all back Judd Walsh, or I'll wash my hands of you for good and all." She was getting hysterical now, and he realised what a complete idiot he would be to let this girl go out of his life; his and her future could take a turn for the better. A new life in a new place; it's what he'd wanted for years. "What do you want me to do Yvonne?" he said resignedly "If you hurry they might still be there, you've been gone less than half an hour, they're probably not even on their second cuppa yet, please try for both our sakes," she said between the sobs.

A rush of adrenalin filled him, and he was all set to go. "I'll drop you off on my way to college," she said. Going the back way and avoiding the carnival, they were at the entrance to the department store in less than three minutes. She quickly kissed him and sped off with tears still in her eyes.

In two minutes he was on his way to the Gents, hoping against hope that the coat was still where he had left it. He pushed the door open; nothing, there was no coat there. Panic was beginning to set in. Take it easy he said to himself, and with a wry smile, you're good at that. Where to now? He began to settle down and think. Maybe somebody's handed it in, Customer information; now where was it? He'd seen it somewhere on his way in the first time. The front door, by the front door; he set off at a run and dabbing the perspiration from his eyes, with his hanky, approached the counter.

"Excuse me miss," he said to the girl on the other side of the counter, (fleetingly thinking no wonder I can't get a job, they're all women who work in these places) "I paid a visit to the Gents about half an hour ago, and left my coat hung on the back of the door, do you know if anyone's handed it in at all?"

Looking nonplussed she said, "I don't know, I've only just started my shift, and then shouting to another girl to the left of her, "Mavis, anybody handed a coat in?"

"About five minutes ago, it's on the stool there beside you," she shouted back. His heart was racing now hurry, hurry, hurry.

"Can you identify it Sir?"

"It's the one you're holding in your hand" he said.

"I'm afraid that's not enough," again, "Sir, what would you say is in the pockets?" she asked.

Thinking on his feet, he replied, "A wallet and a couple of credit cards." "What name would be on the cards Sir?" she asked as she took one out of the wallet checking it carefully.

His mind was in turmoil now, he knew the first name was Bill by the conversation in the café, but the second, what was it? What was it? He'd had a quick glance before he'd returned them to the wallet, "Bill… Jagger" he blurted out, and thank God for the Rolling Stones he thought.

"That's fine Sir," she said, "now be careful with it next time, it looks quite an expensive coat, and it would be a shame to lose it".

On the way out to the street he hastily replaced the notes in the wallet, and the wallet in the inside coat pocket, the gold watch and the change (minus the bus fare from the trip to his flat) into the outer pockets, and set off at a trot.

Now are they still there, he thought as he crossed the road and into the café, the coat behind his back? That damned bell again, attracting attention. His heart gave a leap, the foursome were still there, and still eating and drinking.

Good old Stan, he'd been true to his word, and had got the drinks in again. With his heart beating like a drum at a military tattoo, he made his way to the coat rack in the corner and was six inches away from returning the coat to its hook, when suddenly an ear piercing scream hit the air.

"What are you doing with my Bills coat, put it back", then "Thief; thief," and all hell broke loose, the game was up and he made a dash for the door, only to be confronted by two burly lads from the first table.

"Mr Walsh" said D I Griffith, grabbing Judd by the collar, "let me introduce you to my friend D C Charles Parry. It's amazing what you can pick up in here Charlie, apart from the best cuppa in town: read him his rights." "You'll go down this time Judd. The trouble with you lot is, you never learn, do you."

First Love

It was April when Todd first set eyes on Melissa, it was now the middle of June and they had been seeing each other constantly for over two months now.

It had been a hot sweltering day. Summer was always hot in this part of the South. The party at a mutual friend's house had broken up early and it was too warm to be indoors. "Let's go to lakeside Todd, it will at least be cooler there," and Melissa opened the door; her slim silhouette bathed in the moonlight. Todd viewed her nakedness beneath her summer dress which with her perspiration, was clinging to her body in all the right places. Even after just a short time of knowing her, he knew that he loved her deeply, from the first time she had smiled at him and he had looked into those dark brown eyes.

He had laughed at the idea of love at first sight but now in his case, he knew full well how true it was. "Sure thing Mel" he said and followed her through the door and out into the cooler air.

They ran at first, hand in hand, and then slowed to a walking pace, arms around each other. He turned to her and ever so gently brushed her long flowing hair across her shoulder and lightly kissed her neck, feeling the warmth of her body and tasting the saltiness of her sweat on his lips. They stopped for a short while, arms encircling each other, tightly pressing their young bodies together, there was no feeling at all like the overwhelming feeling of pure love, and they were a million miles away from anyone else, on their own in space and time. "Last one in is a loser" said Mel and broke away from Todd and began running in the direction of the lake.

He watched her gracefulness, as she ran long legged in the moonlight, like a gazelle, a thing of sheer beauty. He let her run on ahead, reminding himself of how young they both were, she was eighteen and he was coming up to twenty in August. It was the first proper relationship for both of them and it seemed that neither wanted anyone else. By the time he got to the lakeside Melissa was frolicking in the water like a nymph, her dress was lying where she had thrown it on the grass. "Come on Todd, it's beautiful in here" she called to him laughingly. Overcoming his awkwardness he stripped down to his shorts and followed her into the coolness of the water. She splashed him and he did the same to her, and they gently pushed each other back into the water, again and again. Each touch of her tanned naked skin was like an electrical charge that went through his hands and burned him deep inside, filling him full of love and longing, for this beautiful girl in front of him.

They had not so far in their brief relationship made love but if there was ever a night just made for it, Todd felt that this was it.

His thoughts were not of pure animal instinct, but something on a par with the angels, then he admonished himself for his stupidity in thinking that way, but it was a feeling of longing and love and closeness, and he so hoped it would be the same for Melissa.

Their tentative splashing and pushing of each other ceased at about the same time as they both realised the spell they were under. He gazed lovingly at her long hair cascading down her back, her slightly turned up nose, her beautiful shoulders and the outline of her young breasts captured in the glow of the moonlight as she turned toward him. He reached out and drew her close to him and she responded immediately with a long passionate kiss on his lips, they each emitted a sigh and drew each other closer still, and after a passionate embrace Todd slipped his arm around her shoulders and she pressed her lips against his neck, then relaxed her head against his shoulder as they made their way to the water's edge, sensually exposing a little more of each other as they made their way to the shallows and on to dry land, stopping every few minutes to taste some more of the fruits of first love.

They lay side by side on the grass and Todd caressed and kissed her face and neck and stroked her hair, she looked on him with a loving smile and softly uttered his name as her fingers danced lazily across his broad shoulders and down his back.

It was the most powerful and fulfilling feeling that either had experienced before.

And it seemed time passed endlessly, filled with caresses and kisses and telling each other straight from the heart exactly how they felt about each other, and what they hoped for the future.

Their love for each other and the sensuality of it all, in this world where only they existed, consumed them and awkwardly for the first time in body, as well as in mind they became as one.

The Music Goes Round And Round

I'm 69 and the only one left; I bear the burden for us all now.

I remember it well. It was 1960, and it was summer. Sunshine filled the days and romance filled the nights. Soft warm nights, too-early ending nights, and before that; long everlasting days. I wax lyrical now but that's only in hindsight.

My mind was in turmoil most of the time. All the love songs that were being sung then were about Marie and me, no doubt about that. I felt it so strongly. A few short months before I had met her at the dance hall, it was all about mates, malarkey and messing around.

But that all changed when this ginger haired beauty of nearly seventeen cast her eyes my way. In fact 'Only Sixteen' a hit song that was doing the rounds at that time summed her up very well.

After a short while I hated Marie with a passion. She played havoc with all our minds; the lads of course. All the camaraderie that we had, had seemed to slip away overnight. Jealousy drove a wedge between us all, and it didn't take long. And she knew what she was doing, oh yes… she knew right enough. She'd played this game before.

And it was a game, we all I think understood that as young as we were, but it made no difference. We were all trapped.

There were four of us lads, and we'd been mates ever since primary school, until now in our late teens when we knew almost everything there was to know about each other.

There was Charlie a rough and tumble lad from a dodgy home. Then there was Steve; he of the fiendish wit, who could have us all in stitches one minute and with his jibes, put you outside the doors of hell itself the next. Then there were Fred and me; brothers with no dad around.

We'd hardly ever had a cross word between us until she came along. She was lovely she was leggy and we all fell head over heels in love with her, and almost instantly became enemies. We'd watch her make a play for each of the others of us. Not brazenly, but behind each other's backs. She'd dazzle us with her smile and she bewitched us all with her charm. Yes she was a witch alright, and deserved her punishment.

The fisticuffs started between Charlie and our Fred some few weeks later; quite harmlessly at first until they got down to the nitty-gritty and mentioned that name. Charlie taunted Fred with it. "Marie wants me not you," he yelled. And Fred punched him in the mouth, splitting his knuckle while knocking out one of Charlie's teeth. "Let's see if she fancies you now?" shouted our Fred. That was the first time that the two of them from being five years old had ever laid a hand on each other.

"Pack it in," I shouted, and pushing between the two got a punch in the ear from Charlie for my troubles.

Then all hell broke loose. All four of were us at it now, friendships built over years disintegrated in less than a few moments.

We were all crazy about her; and she'd made us all crazy.

We were friends for life, the four of us, and we'd intended it to stay that way. No-one was going to split us up like this. But she did; we shunned each other like strangers. None of us collected under the lampposts to chat and laugh as before. And none of us got the girl. She spurned each and every one of us in turn, picked someone else and mocked us all in passing.

It maybe wouldn't have mattered so much if she hadn't pushed our noses in it, but she had, and along with the fact that we were all insanely jealous now, we looked for revenge.

The four of us lads were back on the same wave length now, and concentrated all our energies on vengeance. It would be bonfire night in a few weeks, the summer having come and gone, and we meant to deal a terrifying blow to this girl who had bewitched us all and left us the worse for it. We watched and waited until we found the time to strike.

It was just after dark on the 5th and the four of us planned to truss her up and deposit her in exchange for the guy on the biggest bonfire on the spare ground at the end of our street. Half an hour waiting in terrified silence for the fire to be lit would deal her a lesson she'd never forget.

Six pm and the deed was done and no-one any the wiser. All of us now would go for our tea and be back before the bonfire was lit at the usual time of 7pm.

Half an hour later Fred noticed that it was raining lightly; a drizzle, hardly enough to run off our greasy hair, and we strolled down to the end of the street lighting a ciggie apiece. We met up with Charlie and Steve on the way and talked of how genuinely pleased Marie would be for once, to see us. We turned the last corner and on to the croft with enough time to free her before the appointed hour.

The wood had really caught fire quite rapidly. The recent forecast was for rain and Tommy Harrison's dad whose turn it was to light the fire that year had begun the proceedings early while the wood was still dry. Nothing could be seen or heard except for the roaring flames. We four stood there in complete disbelief.

We have never uttered a word of it from that day to this and the thing I recall with most clarity was a record player booming out through somebody's window; part of the verse from an Elvis record… 'Marie's the name of his Latest Flame,' it chills me still.

The whole area was cleared the next day by the council and was deposited on the local landfill site, and within a few short months was buried forever.

A Walk in the Park

Killing me was easy, just one karate chop and my neck was broken. Then he pushed me down the stairs to make it look like an accidental death. He'd got Delia now and my money. But I'll get my own back.

I've always been lucky; but it's not hereditary 'cos the rest of my family used to rub their knuckles on my head for good luck, and I became bald at a very early age. Nothing wrong with being follically challenged, but at thirteen it's a bit much; yet I digress. The fact of the matter was that I was now dead. It was just six stairs, from my den to the lounge area, but accidental or otherwise it came to the same thing. All the work that I'd put in over the years, from serving tables in a 'greasy spoon' on the Bowery's lower east side, to top chef and then owner of a chain of restaurants across the States and to this beautiful apartment in Manhattan, had been brought to a conclusive end by of all things a karate chop, and I was a vegetarian. I was on one side of the curtain and my wife and her lover and most of all, my money, were on the other side.

Amazingly it didn't look much of a barrier from where I was standing but it might just as well have been a fifty foot wall. A one-sided transparent wall, as I was pretty sure that they couldn't see me, but still a wall, and it was quite fascinating to watch as the two murderers, (they were both in it together,) connived and plotted frantically as to what to do next. Georgie Porgy as I called him had been a friend; a heck of a lot friendlier to Delia than to me it now seemed. He was bathed in a pool of sweat that was running profusely from under his carefully coiffed hairpiece, (I always went au natural myself,) down his face and around his size nineteen collar and then to regions best known to Delia and most of the slappers in Manhattan. Some of his perspiration fell on Delia's face and, just, just for a moment, it looked like she was crying, but with the smile on her face at the knowledge that I had breathed my last and that my money was now within her grasp, the two emotions seemed strange bedfellows. Money was George's big love; anybody's, and it was the same with my widow; as I shall have to get used to referring to her. So at least they had that in common.

Crazy as it may sound, I wasn't the least bit bothered. I didn't feel any different being dead although it seemed odd I'm sure you'll agree, on seeing myself in a crumpled heap at the bottom of the stairs with my leg wrapped at a crazy angle round the newel post. I had nearly been in that position once or twice before, after an evening in with my friend Jack Daniels. But I'd never been that quiet for that long, not with a face that colour anyway.

Needless to say one look was enough; it could upset my appetite. And then I wondered whether I still had one, (an appetite I mean,) although the other thought had crossed my mind as well. I suppose I should have been glad to be in one piece as it were, regardless of whether everything was functioning or not.

Then I left them to their talk of money, their careful planning of the story of my demise, my money, and my insurance. Now, there would lay a dime or three. I was never in any doubt that I would financially be better off dead, but now I was definitely certain of one thing… they were.

It seemed more like an order than a request to me, and it sounded more like a thought than an actual voice. But it was there filling my head with its insistence for me to be somewhere other than I now was. I followed where it led. Down and down I went thinking vaguely to myself, shouldn't I be going the other way? And boy was it getting warmer. I hadn't had the time or the inclination to take note of whatever outward appearance I may have had, but cooked sausage and eggs came to mind as I glanced down at my lower lumbar regions and discovered I was totally void of covering. There is a two word expression that identifies exactly what I am trying to say, but for the death of me I can't think of it. Downward I continued, enclosed somehow in an ever descending spiral, and on the way passing people of all shapes and sizes. At first all those I passed were as myself, short of a decent wardrobe, and let me tell you as I sped past some of those of the particularly surgically enhanced, I searched in vain for a pause button, but no luck… you do realise I was speaking of luscious ladies, yeah?

It got a little less interesting as I realised that they were all at work of some kind or another and the further down I went the more clothes appeared on the perspiring bodies and the harder the work appeared. My conveyance came to a sudden halt and I fell forward like a crash test dummy.

A huge sweating corpulent mass of a man threw at my feet a set of thermal under clothes the like of which my Granddaddy used to wear, six shirts two sweaters and a tie, three suits of clothes and a great grey heavy woollen overcoat, all the right size to be fitted one on top of the other and all brand spanking new. And to finish off the ensemble a massive pair of what could only be described as diver's boots, the weight of which led me to believe that in some invisible way the diver was still in them;

and he was a big fella. 'Sign here,' said the bloated blob, offering me a clipboard.

To cut a long story short, I was in this Hellhole, for brother that's where we all of us were, H, E double L, HELL, for what seemed an indescribable amount of time, feeding the fiery furnaces, day and night, night and day. I half expected Francis Albert Sinatra to stroll by singing that particular lyric, but it never happened, not at least while I was there anyhow. No booze but all the food you could eat, not exactly a Holiday Inn and for some time I thought that the cuisine was part of the torture, which by the way I didn't think I rightly deserved. Don't get me wrong I had been no angel but I hadn't been one of the bad guys either.

Then one day it happened; something that must have gotten lost in the post or whatever had finally arrived and found its way onto the boss's desk. Well there they were; my credentials, I was just the guy they were looking for; top chef, chain of restaurants; the works. It came to my notice that because of the delay the boss was fuming, which by the way wasn't hard for him to do, and I was despatched post haste to Hell's Kitchen.

The idea was that I would improve no end the culinary aspects of the place and restore some kind of savour to the menu at unknown times and unexpectedly so that from the lowest, (and there were some pretty low characters in there,) to the highest, (and to those, ordinarily bad BO would have been a fragrance to be desired,) they could enjoy something that would instil in the minds of the dwellers therein, a comparison to show just how badly off they were.

What's Hell without knowing you're in there?

I got my instructions on how to find my way there by some guy, who it seemed to me on reflection, must have had in his previous existence the directional sense of a bloodhound with an exceptionally bad cold. I was suitably attired and sent on my way; three doors down, up forty two levels in the elevator, second right and follow your nose.

As I entered through the double doors it appeared as if my whole being had come in contact with and emerged through, a great Perspex sheet which had stretched thinner and thinner until I had burst through in a matter of seconds. I was left standing, my eyes blinking and taking in a sight that I had not seen since my early days in the Bowery.

If this was the place, it was indeed a welcome change in more ways than one, the tips were great too. I may not have gone to Law School but I had the sense after some little lapse in time to know that this now was not Hell. I'd been sent to the wrong place, but those were the orders and here I was. This was Hell's Kitchen alright but Hell's Kitchen which in Realtors terminology was now known as Clinton and Mid-town West, but was still Hell's Kitchen to the native New Yorker. I ditched my apron and picked a coat off of a peg and to use a colloquial term, I was outta there.

From 39th and 7th I found my way to Central Park and crossed over a corner of it; what a beautiful day for a walk in the Park, and on to East 68th Street and my apartment at 627. The commissionaire looked me up and down, thought he vaguely recognised me, (I'd lost quite some weight, languishing in Hell,) as being a resident and opened the door wide. Two others, apparently tourists, took his attention away from me and I entered the elevator and before he had probably turned around was knocking on the door of my apartment.

'Hello, who is it?' The voice of Georgie Porgy squeaked from behind the solid oak door as I turned my head away from the spy hole that gave a view of the corridor in which I was standing. He would have been able just see the back of my bald head, and having not long before positioned his toup' delicately upon his own somewhat empty head adopted a happy smile of superiority and without waiting for an answer, opened the door. At least his last moments before he caught sight of my face were happy; then he clutched his chest gave a gurgling sound as if he'd just let out the last of the bath water, which he most certainly had, clutched again this time at the door in an attempt to close it and expired on the welcome mat.

'You're welcome,' I said quietly and bundled him back through the door and inside, closing the door behind me.

'Who was it honey?' she asked as she appeared at the bathroom door dressed in her skin. Delia had been lovely once and the signs were still there, but now wasn't the time and as I shrugged thoughtfully, deemed that it never would be again. I got her to reveal the whereabouts of 'my' insurance money; all in cash by the way… they were just about to embark on a cruise. '*WE* could go now,' she said pleadingly but I declined the offer and strangled her instead. I dragged old, but not getting any older Georgie on top of her, it was probably his favourite position anyway, and arranged his hands in such a way as to appear that he'd cut off her air supply immediately before succumbing to the vengeance of an altogether higher power, which in this case had been me. I really must stop these delusions of grandeur, but it comes with the territory. I couldn't be blamed; I was already dead and buried and now I'd got the insurance money to prove it.

I slept in the refrigerator for the next couple of nights just to acclimatise myself, and then with my money my passport and nothing other than that in which I had arrived I made a stealthy exit.

Two days later I was sitting under a parasol in the south of France with a female of the species, drinking a glass of cool white wine to keep down the temperature. It seemed that the after effects of living in Hell were slowly wearing off, it had been far too hot for me anyway, and maybe this was Heaven … and then again… maybe not.

Matthew 7:15

He'd set out at a good walking pace and had made his way across the fields by way of the winding lanes edged with the ivy covered grey stone walls and was now about a half mile into the densely packed forest. At first the trees had been little more than saplings with reddened leaves curling up now and then as he passed, and falling to the forest floor to join the carpet already laid there by their elder brothers and sisters. "If that was the way of things?" he said aloud and at the same time feeling quite glad that there was no-one about to hear him voice his thoughts.

It had been a sunny yet cold start to the day, but he was well wrapped up against the autumnal weather. The sun at first sight had given the appearance of a beautiful day to come, but as he knew appearances could sometimes be deceptive. The bright sunlight shone through the gaps in the foliage overhead and dappled the ground in front of him and made for a pleasant walk, so pleasant that at times he broke into a disjointed whistle of a tune he could never remember properly, but which he forced through his tortured lips anyway.

Slowly and surely he had been walking up a slight gradient and pushing through the lighter of the lower branches and forging on resolutely to the summit of the incline, the way which was now getting steeper with each pronounced tread. He reached the top of the climb and stepped over the moss covered ridge, lost his balance, and his feet and legs took on a life of their own as he began an unstoppable race downhill and onward through a small clearing. His headlong rush was only brought to a halt by the first of the trees at the next outcrop of new growth in the further part of the forest which he hit full on, and from which he crumpled and fell senseless to the ground.

How long he had been caught there in the lowest branches of the tree, he had no idea, but he was quite cold now and no sign of the sun could he see, although it was still not dark, but cloud covered. His head was hurting and he touched his fingers to his face and felt the crustiness of dried blood on his temple and a, sore to the touch rather large, bump. He was sore all over. He dragged himself hand over hand, up the tree by its branches, some catching his face and making him pull back his head in pain. He stood erect and as soon as he relaxed his weight upon his weary limbs, his right foot immediately gave way beneath him and he fell forward and cursed aloud as he crashed through the undergrowth and lay prone amongst the roots and leaves that covered the forest floor.

Spitting out the grass and dirt that had entered his open mouth as he had landed face down, he thought he heard a sound, just a slight noise as if some nocturnal animal or bird might make on readying itself for the start of the hunt for its prey, in the now rapidly darkening surroundings. He could not even show a light as he had no survival kit of any kind.

"Just going for a walk," he had said to Mrs Potts the Landlady at the small B&B where he was staying for the week, as he was on the way out of the door.

"Don't forget dinner's served at five thirty, on the dot," she had reminded him, "roast beef and all the trimmings."

If he had told her once, he must have told her forty times he was a vegetarian.

He started again, as he heard the sound being repeated, this time closer than before, and he strained his eyes to see into the enveloping darkness. A figure of sorts ran past his line of vision and he stopped himself short of calling out. He had no way of knowing whether it was man or beast and he thought it best not to direct too much attention to his presence. He tried once more to gain his feet, and this time succeeded, as a gap appeared in the clouds and the moonlight played down upon him.

In full view now of the creator of the sounds that had disturbed his self pitying assessment of his injuries, a shadowy figure advanced toward him behind the beam of a flash-light.

"I say lost are we?" called out the squeaky voice of Mr Tweed his fellow B&B-er as he pushed his face almost into his face, and shone his flash-light up his nose."I thought I saw you ahead of me earlier, I meant to call out but you were too far away."

And he then proceeded to inform the suffering walker of every twist and turn that he had taken along the path that had brought him to this very place including the boat trip and then the train journey from his home on an island somewhere off some unpronounceable part of the Scottish mainland. Verbose was not the word, why use one when twenty would do? He didn't like this little man, who had driven him almost to distraction in the small accommodation in which they could hardly be any distance apart, and his conversations were a bore; he could talk a glass eye to sleep.

He was a nasty piece of work as well. On the odd occasion when he was quiet he seemed always to be up to something. He had been spotted on several occasions returning to the communal lounge from private areas of the house in which he had no leave to be. His meals were never as they should have been; his aged mother (who he had left at home to fend for herself) was a far better cook than Mrs Potts, he had told everybody, except the lady in question of course. He didn't go that far, he would much rather make the bullets and hope somebody else fired them. As it was the ever punctilious landlady was as good a cook as any of the four other guests could expect her to be, being on her own the Head cook and bottle washer.

After some thirty minutes or more of listening to Tweed the weed's diatribe he attempted again to put some weight on his right foot and found to his surprise that it held up incredibly well, in fact his movement was quite supple, and he made a point of standing on the one leg, then turning his ankle this way and that, and felt remarkably fit.

The clouds scudded across the sky again and revealed the full moon in all its majesty, and as he knew from past experience that they would, his eyes felt rather heavy and lupine, his features changed dramatically, his teeth grew sharper and ever longer and he leaned across to Mr Tweed's petrified rigid form with his rapidly extending finger nailed hairy hands, drew him closer and sank his fangs into his neck.

Mr Tweed said nary a word but slumped to the ground stone dead.

To be truthful there wasn't an almighty lot of meat on the bones, and what there was of it was quite stringy, but it filled a hole as they say. He buried the bones and the clothes, rescued the torch to find his way well clear of the forest and back to the B&B, and then threw it into a deep pond some distance from the cottage.

"Mr Lamb, you've missed dinner," called Mrs Potts as he crossed the dining hall to make his way up to his room to check on his lumps and bumps.

"That's okay Mrs Potts," he replied patting his stomach, "I've already eaten."

It was only occasionally that he ate meat, and this had just happened to be one of those times.

(Nb:...they come to you in sheep's clothing but inwardly are ravening wolves Matthew 7:15)

The Magic Island

In the midst of the Pacific Ocean and a thousand miles from the nearest land mass lies the fabled Isle of Havau Bina. This small floating coral reef in the azure sea is in no particular place on any map, and has been known throughout time to be in as many oceans as there are around these lands of ours, and not just confined to one.

This island set in the silver sea is the home of the Garbled Nark, a kind and benevolent beast of great stature and peaceful demeanour who would be seized with dismay at the mere thought of being considered a *beast.* There was not a finer being for many a league, or even seven; and he had the boots to prove it. Had it not been he who had paddled this island all the way through storm and mountainous seas to the other side of the seaward sound to rescue the good witch Hetta and her band of followers from the clutches of Eldon the Merciless, the three headed troll? Had it not been he who had heard the whisper in the wind that had taken him alone to Algart to save the False Princess with the big nose called Suhna, (the princess, not the nose,) and bring her and her beloved, back to the peace of this fabled Isle? And was it not he alone who was King without subjects, in this lush and verdant land?

He was not alone on this mystic atoll although to the rest of the islanders he was not there at all. He was considered a myth; a figment of the imagination; a something that somebody saw after they had partaken of too much of the intoxicating brani, a drink made from the root of the brand-new tree, which had only recently been discovered. They had no idea why their island was, for some time in the most clement of climes, and then overnight as it were, set down amid the snowy seas and ice-floes populated with the Lesser Spotted Admiral bird, native to such monochrome lands, exchanging not one wit of conversation, but standing to attention and peering intently as they passed each other on the high seas.

These unaware islanders of Havau Bina put it down to the changing of the seasons and thought no more of it.

But the Garbled Nark who called himself Tony, ('cos he was t'on'y one of his kind on t' island) sat upon the highest point and looked down upon the comings and goings of these dwellers. On the east of the island lived the Neffas who were ignorant of the Twains who lived in the west, yet was it not said that east is east and west is west and Neffa the Twain shall meet; but they hadn't. Well not until tomorrow anyway. Tomorrow would be another day, as it usually is of course.

Tomorrow being Wednesday and half- day closing, was not usually a busy day, but at one-o-clock, as the crow flies, a large, if not gargantuan raft appeared on the horizon. Six-a-breast and two high were the occupants of this bringer of ill fortune, shading their eyes from the sun whilst attempting to get a closer look at what was before them.

"Looks like the shops are shut," a voice from the front said whose owner had a better view than the rest.

"Don't let that put us off," said another, with rank and filed teeth, "Maybe we can do some cannibalising? It's a while since we had breakfast."

So the dastardly dozen paddled their oars, (or words to that effect,) and made land in no time at all.

Tony of course was sitting in his usual position, which could be quite painful at times, for when the sun was off it, the cold stone wasn't such a blessing on his haemorrhoids, which also brought back memories of Emma Royd who had jilted him when he was a teenager, and the pain was still there. From his vantage point high above the island he saw that the invaders had landed smack dab in the centre of the east and west territories, and amid such scurrying to and fro of the inhabitants of the ocean oasis as had never before been seen, the Neffas and the Twains caught sight of each other for the first time and of course the prophecy regarding the east and west has now come true.

The Neffas, (fight? You're joking,) was never a combative force and their being only two hundred or so, they were no match for the invaders, being a full twelve in number. And the Twains weren't much better on account of they kept splitting in two and going in different directions.

Well there was nothing for it, but that Tony had to take a hand.

So he took out his Visible cloak which he hadn't seen for years and for the life of him couldn't imagine why, and brandishing a length of Pampas grass which grew quite abundantly thereabouts, threw himself down the hill, then picked himself up, dressed his wounds; in a nice little pink number, and carried on down to confront the foe. The sight of this Garbled Nark dressed to kill and waving its pampas grass, was more than the intruders could face, having yet had nothing to drink and therefore not soused enough to pick up any old floozy; and the force turned and fled, never to return.

Both the Neffas and the Twains were joined in unison, but came apart later for a celebratory drink whilst proclaiming Tony the

King of the island, which of course he already was, he had just not been seen to be, because he hadn't worn his Visible cloak before. The good witch Hetta and her band played Wings, 'Band on the Run,' and they all laughed as they rushed back and forth to the toilets all night. Hetta later made out that it was only a spell, but it seemed like all night to the band.

The Princess Suhna married her beloved, (sooner him than me,) and they all lived happily ever after, or as happily ever after, as a great hulking Ogre, two tribes of idiots, a witch, her coven, and a big nosed pretend Princess and her Prince could, on an island, with no work, no money, no wireless and no telly.

No flies on George

George had been standing there, just inside the foyer of this rather plush hotel, for getting on for thirty minutes now. He'd been a few minutes late as he couldn't find a parking space, and had had to walk quite a way. The hotel was a little above his class if truth were known but he was suited and booted and didn't look in any way as if he shouldn't be there. He was trying to make a good impression and thought Tommy Cooper might go down well; then he checked himself. For goodness sake act your age man; it was all nerves of course. It had been a while since George had been in the company of a lady and he wanted all to go well. He didn't really know whether there was any dress code these days, after all it didn't seem that long ago that he'd seen a picture of one of the ex Beatles wearing a suit and a pair of trainers; and McCartney was the same age as himself. Of course there was a *little* difference in their financial situation but George hoped that it wasn't too obvious.

There was a time just a short while ago when he had thought of having his grey hair dyed and cut into a more trendy style, but then he had said to himself, "what the heck, if they don't like me as I am they can always look elsewhere," he talked a lot to himself these days. It was warm and he was perspiring a little, he didn't know whether to take a seat further inside the foyer, but then immediately dismissed the idea. If she didn't see him face on she was sure not to recognise him. But she did have the advantage (if that's what you'd call it,) of having seen a recent photograph of him; a head shot facing the camera, but George had no idea what *she* looked like in the slightest.

Looking back into the foyer he saw about another dozen or so people sitting about the place on quite comfortable leather couches. Most were couples involved in chatting amicably husband to husband wife to wife, there were three youngish looking girls,(mind you everyone looked young to George these days,) and what looked like a very classy lady, way out of Georges league; a former model by what he could see of her style and dress. She was immersed in some magazine or other, and it must have been of great interest as she seemed oblivious of her surroundings and never flinched as he came through the door. There were also four rugby types who were acting like kids trying to catch the eyes of the three young girls. One of the lads was going to be disappointed George thought, as he turned and resumed his watch upon the entrance.

The attraction of the lady he had come to see had been enhanced by her profile; she seemed like a good sort and added to that was the description of herself as being 'curvy,' but as the minutes ticked by the thought entered his mind that that may not mean what he thought it might; not Jayne Mansfield or Marilyn Monroe but possibly Mr Blobby.

He was wondering now rather nervously whether to make a break for it while he still had the chance. His shirt was soaking now with panic driven sweat, he lifted his arms up and down in an attempt to allow some fresh air to flow, and he looked above his head just to see if there were any swarms of flies hanging around as he thought there surely must have been. He was clear on that count, but he was attracting some rather odd glances from the commissionaire, if that's what they called them these days. In the thirty minutes of standing mostly in the same position, he had begun to realise that he was actually waiting there for someone who for all he knew might be the exact opposite of the lady in his imagination. The accumulation of his distinctly worsening body odour and the dread that his recent review of what may be in store for him proved too much for him to endure. George made a beeline for the revolving door and extricated himself from the situation; at least he would live to fight another day, maybe with a snapshot as a guide.

This was the trouble with this online dating, if you hadn't seen a photo you just didn't know what you were up against. He'd tried his best to be as truthful as he could be. He was divorced, a pensioner on a limited income, had most of his own hair, anyone could see on the photo that he was going thin at the front, and he had a covered over bald patch at the back which would be hardly noticeable, as he was quite a bit taller than the ladies on the dating site who all seemed to be in the region of five feet two or three. He'd tried to come across as being sincere and he thought he'd managed it quite well. He'd had e-mails from a good number of ladies, (he'd even had one from a fella, which he'd instantly blocked,) but most lived a hundred miles or more away.

It had been nearly ten years since George had been divorced and he'd had a couple of relationships since but they had come to nothing after he'd wined and dined them and taken them away on holiday and they had spent most of his money. It seemed to be a career for some of these women, not quite the oldest profession; but near enough he thought. He then spent a couple of years on his own with just his cat for company until he'd seen the advert on TV. He'd never been influenced by any advert in his life, and those on TV, well he usually turned the sound off when they interrupted the programme.

It was a well made advert; boy meets girl and all that. It was quite likely that it was just good timing, he'd been waiting for a jolt; maybe this was it. After all he thought, it couldn't do him any harm. He got his laptop out and reminded himself how to get on the internet, he'd taken an I.T. course at the local tech a couple of years before and he found it was just like riding a bike. He subscribed to broadband so he may as well use it. A quick look through his files and he had got it sorted, what was that about an old dog and new tricks?...rubbish. Thirty quid for three months, he was happy with that especially if it brought results. There were plenty of ladies to look at and some of their profiles made quite interesting reading and there were those the sight of which made him wish he was twenty years younger. It seemed recently as if time was passing him by at an accelerating speed, and he certainly missed female companionship, he wasn't an unromantic person and there was still some fire left in the engine room.

After a number of false starts he had come across this lady's profile. A nice name Janine he thought. He could do a lot worse he thought, in another bout of thinking, and she only lived less than ten miles away. It was his suggestion that they meet at the Imperial, after all it was the swankiest place for miles around. Was that even a word he thought? Anyway regardless; he'd arrived a little late due to the difficulties of finding a parking slot and he thought he looked the part, whether anybody else did remained to be seen.

Janine had been a looker in her day and she was still a lady to get ones heart pounding. She had the fine cheekbones of a model and lips generous, smiling and inviting. As a teenager she could have been a double for Elizabeth Taylor, but that was a long time ago now. The surprising thing about her was that she had never taken her looks as anything but God given; she had never been a show off or a vamp. She was good hearted and had had a fine marriage. She and her husband John had been married for thirty four years until his death five years before. That had been a terrible time for Janine, apart from a small number of close friends she was on her own. She had never been able to have children and although it had come as a shock at first, both John and she involved themselves in other things.

She would be sixty four years old in September, a week after which would have been their fortieth anniversary. Since the death of her husband she had joined various organisations, ladies, ladies and more ladies. She was aching for the arm of a gentleman to lean upon.

Her very best and oldest friend, Rebecca had brought her the newspaper advert and she had said, "Janine you'll have to make the break sometime, there's a knight in shining armour out there just waiting to meet you and carry you off to his castle." Very poetic was Becky when the mood struck her. So Janine had been talked, or more or less commandeered into signing up for 'Make a Date.' She had taken some advice from someone who had a little experience of such things in that she should never put her photograph on the site. "In what I know of these dating sites," said her neighbour Cheryl, who by the way knew exactly nothing other than what she'd read in the more lurid lower market end of the Sunday tabloids. "There are some rather shady characters that on seeing a pretty face regardless of what age will send e- mails of the basest kind." Janine in no way wanted that.

All she wanted was a gentleman on a level with John and she knew that that would be a tall order. Janine had perused the site for weeks with no success until one day she came across a new member in this game of chance, which she had not ever really wanted to be a part of. She was attracted to him straight away;

something about his smile or the sparkle in his eyes. She couldn't quite put her finger on it, but throwing caution to the wind she sent him an e- mail. His user name DODGER had seemed quite comical and she was intrigued to find out more. She had apologised for contacting him first, she had no idea whether that was the right procedure or not. He had replied with a humorous account; almost an autobiography which had her laughing out loud, something she hadn't done for it seemed an awful long time. Two or three more e- mails from one to the other, and he; his name was George by the way, had suggested they meet up for a meal at a most impressive hotel. She had replied and said that a coffee in a café would do just for a chat, but he was insistent.

Her friend Rebecca had said. "It's probably a good thing, the more people the better; just in case he's the wrong sort." Now the doubts crept in. "One never knew," she had said, which had been a little off putting for Janine. But there really was something that she liked about George, he came across as solid and reliable and she was prepared to take the risk, as small as she thought it might be.

She had some nice clothes, something John had always ensured she had plenty of; anything he bought her at times seemed like a substitute for the children she had never had. Janine picked out a medium low cut burgundy dress and shoes to match, a simple necklace topped everything off. She glanced in the mirror as all ladies do and saw that all was well; she had had her hair styled for the occasion. It was a big step forward for her, and she thought probably for George too, unless he was a serial dater. The thought gave her butterflies in her stomach.

Janine called a cab and arrived there a little before the intended time and settled herself down on one of the plush settees set around the foyer area and proceeded to read a magazine. She lived in a modest semi-detached house herself but was quite happy to read 'Celebrity Homes' Although no great lover of celebrities they did own some beautiful houses, she had no idea how long she'd been absorbed in the magazine, but she suddenly embraced reality again and the reason why she was where she was, and her eyes glanced around her and then to the revolving door. Apart from the people who had been in the room prior to her seating herself on the settee, there was but one man as close to the doors as he could get, intent on watching the people passing by on the pavement outside. He looked quite smart from the back with a nice well pressed grey suit and black shiny shoes.

That was something you didn't see too much of these days, what had happened to the smart way of dressing that had been prevalent in her younger days. Now everyone seemed to dress as if they were going to a barbecue and some looked as if they'd come directly from one. It wasn't just a changing world it had already changed, and for the worse and she was sure George would agree. But then she had to meet George to ask him that.

She was intrigued now by the antics of the man by the door. She smiled to herself. Was he trying to fly; he was lifting his arms up and down slowly at first and then elbows out like a chicken, faster still. The action only lasted for a minute or two, but nearly had her laughing out loud. Oh, if only George were here to see it, she was sure he also would find it hilarious. Then the thought suddenly struck Janine that maybe the man was George. Judging by his humorous e- mails he was capable of doing anything for a laugh, she stood and took a pace or two from her seat in his direction and then she noticed him lifting his head and scanning the area above him wildly, perhaps she was taking too much of a chance. Even the commissionaire was taking note of his actions as well.

She quietly retained her seat and watched as the stranger pushed on the revolving door and exited the hotel. Still it would be a nice comical ice breaker to start the evening. Time had stood still for her, when she put her literary head on she could be completely engrossed in the printed word. Janine picked up the magazine and resumed her reading. George would be along any minute of that she was quite sure.

Something in return

It was mid September and the weather was turning cooler, especially toward the close of the day. There had been an Indian summer, but now it was on the way back from whence it came. India I suppose, thought Michael as he walked along hand in hand with Lorraine. It had been a funny old year; he had followed her from Paris to Rome and then to Spain and back again to Paris. It was a beautiful city, a city made for romance but still she wasn't happy there and today found them walking through the centre of Manchester.

"Tell me again, Lorraine what did we come back here for?" 'Because it's my home and I get homesick from time to time' 'I think if it was my home I'd get sick of it as well; only joking love; but it is quite different than the places we've been backwards and forwards to these last twelve months.' 'There's such a feeling of belonging Michael, and familiarity with everything around me. From the Mancunian accent to the smell of the river Irwell; from Piccadilly to the Town Hall and Central Library, and the Shambles pub. Do you know that a few years back they lifted the whole kit and caboodle of that old inn in one piece and reset it down just a few hundred yards away?

'Wery Interesting,' he said in a mock German accent, and she slapped him playfully on the back of his head. 'Besides there's my family as well; dad and mum and Janine and Freddy, after a while I start to miss them all. It's different for you love having no family of your own, but I really look forward to seeing them again. I'll introduce you to everyone and we'll all go down the local for a knees up.' 'So they call it a knees up in this part of the country as well do they?' asked Michael. 'They call it anything they want as long as everyone has a good time. You southerners can't have it all you know, Mother Brown.' said Lorraine. 'Who's Mother Brown then?' said Michael a frown spreading across his handsome face. 'The one who's forever having a knees up, as you Londoners keep singing on about.' 'I'll never understand your northern humour,' he said. 'Just stick with me our kid,' she replied.

She was an attractive and heart- warming girl and he knew that if he got the chance, he certainly would. He'd met her in Paris and took to her straight away, he'd thought she was French with her long black hair and somewhat Gallic features; it was in her genes she said, 'from way back.'

It was getting on for three in the afternoon when they eventually arrived at Lorraine's parent's house on the edge of a great rambling council estate Michael noticed that the house was nicely painted and the garden was really pleasant, something he hadn't expected when Lorraine had told him where they lived. Dad must be a keen gardener he thought and a bit of a miracle man to keep it the condition that it was in, he even had a small orchard tucked away in the corner of the garden, a pear tree or two by the look of it and an apple tree that Lorraine had said was her dad's pride and joy, lovingly nurtured and cared for by him.

The front door swung open and the whole family as one unit surrounded them all shouting and talking as one. 'Whoa Whoa,' shouted Lorraine's dad as if trying to bring to a stop a stampede of stallions. 'Let them breathe for goodness sake, give 'em air, and immediately sought out Lorraine and gave her a great bear hug that nearly crushed her and made redundant the statement he had just uttered.

'Come in, come in,' said mum; 'put the kettle on our Janine, I bet they could do with a brew.' "And me,' shouted Freddy. 'There's no show without punch is there Fred,' said dad, 'you go and help Janine and don't break any more mugs, you're supposed to drink out of them not throw them at each other.' 'How come I get the women's work?' said Freddy, with his tousled unkempt hair giving him the appearance of just getting out of bed. "Any work at all would be an improvement," butted in his mum, and they all tumbled into the house in a happy mood.

Michael was taken aback by the speed of it all; one minute they had been standing at the front door reflecting quietly on the state of the garden and the house, and the next thing they'd been set upon by this band who it seemed had been intent on taking the very breath from their bodies and rendering them lifeless on the ground at the very least, and within two minutes, with their feet hardly even having touched the floor they were plonked on a settee in the lounge and force fed tea and biscuits. If this is a northern homecoming, Michael thought I dread to know what happens when they're saying goodbye.

'And Michael what is your claim to fame?' said Lorraine's mum. 'Well Mrs Williams…' 'Janet's my name love; I save the Mrs 'til when I'm talking to the council about the yobs round here,' and paused as Michael continued.' 'I haven't really got a claim to fame, I studied Art and Languages at University and it was in Paris that I met Lorraine and we've been together for just about a year now, I'm twenty six, free and single.'

'Eh those were the days lad;' said her husband with a comical sigh, as Janet peered over her glasses at him. 'That'll do James we don't want any of your reminiscing thank you.' 'Anyway' said James following Janet's lead on the use of first names. 'I'm

Jimmy; have that cuppa Michael and I'll show you round the garden, are you a gardener by any stretch of the imagination?' 'Not really… er… Jimmy' said Michael, 'mum tended to it when I was at home, but since she passed away and I went off to Uni, the house has been sold and I've not had a garden of my own since, but I do like to see a colourful display of flowers. They make the house seem so much brighter.'

'Testicles!' said Jimmy, 'I only do the flowers for 'er… ahem... Janet, it's the trees that are my thing, fruit trees, you know. Flowers are only good to look at, but trees; like fruit trees, well, they give you something in return for all the care and attention you lavish on 'em.' 'You've got him started now Michael, he'll be talking about those damn trees 'til the barman shouts time'

'That's an idea,' said Jimmy, 'are we going for a few drinks to embarrass the lass and welcome her boyf… Michael, and Janet, it'll save you washing up as well if we have a bar meal at the same time?

'You can see now why I've been with him all these years, Michael, he's so concerned about my welfare; washing up indeed, I don't think *you* even know where the pots go, lad. Get back to your trees Tarzan!" "You see what it is lad I've got this prize Golden Delicious, and I got my first lot of apples from it this year and I've great hopes for it. It's got the best spot for the best of the weather and it's nicely sheltered.'

'Lorraine mentioned it to me on the way in,' said Michael trying to get a word in edgewise; 'I suppose it'll take some time to get it well established.' 'Not with my hands at t' tiller sunshine, I'll have it up and going in no time at all; I mix my own food for my little orchard and before long I'll have the biggest and best apples and pears for miles around.'

'Are we going out?' said Freddy. 'What's your hurry lad you're only just old enough to get in the pub?' said his mother. 'And' butted in Janine, 'he has to take an I D card with him to prove it; such a sweet little baby face.' 'LEAVE THAT MUG ON THE TABLE LAD,' said his father slowly, catching Freddie's intention out of the corner of his eye; "that one's going to be washed."

'Janet was right about what she had said earlier, Jimmy was still talking about his trees when the pub closed their doors behind them. Michael had had some respite whilst being introduced to friends and neighbours, and laughs and jokes were bandied backwards and forwards, and drinks were spilled and people fell off their chairs. A typical Saturday night by all accounts, but it all ended good humouredly. And as soon as everyone broke up Jimmy was back to his trees again. Michael sent out a telepathic message to Lorraine to come and rescue him but his message was blocked by her mother's questioning of her regarding the state of the relationship between the two lovers.

'Really mum it's fine, we get on extremely well and… it's just fine at the moment, neither of us is looking for anyone else and we're both just happy to see where it leads.' 'I'm really glad for both of you love, and he seems such a nice man.' 'Trust me mum I wouldn't pick any other kind.' Mum put her arm around her and started humming the wedding march softly in Lorraine's ear and they both laughed. Freddy and Janine hurried on to get home first to put the kettle on. They'd actually volunteered which came as a great surprise to their mother who said. 'Well there's a first time for everything I suppose,' and then, 'WATCH THEM MUGS.'

'Bloody hell Janine; what's dad going to say when he sees this.'

The vandalised trees were strewn in broken branches and littered leaves across the width of the road and four or five of the small privets that had been part of the hedge that had surrounded the garden had been uprooted as well. It was a disaster area; and dad's laughter ceased as he approached the carnage. 'I can't believe that anyone could sink that low,' he said. His shoulders slumped; and except for Michael's intervention he most probably would have collapsed on the spot. 'They're bloody animals; bloody animals, said Janet in tears. 'These yobs can't understand the meaning of happy, except to go all out and smash it to smithereens and then laugh about it, what have they achieved apart from breaking a man's heart? They've no idea about the hours of care and attention and love that's been given…oh I don't know why I bother, it's hopeless, what chance have we got; the police don't care, they just let them run riot. This place is going from bad to worse.' She sank down with her head in her hands, and Lorraine picked her up and held her close.

'I didn't think things were this bad mum? And here was me boasting to Michael about all the good things I was missing about this place, and then he witnesses something like this.' 'It's not all the kids love, it's just a bad crowd who drag others in with them; I blame the parents, some of them are worse than the kids.

Mrs Williams got in touch with the council the first thing Monday morning but all they could say was, 'It's really a matter for the police Mrs Williams, there's no damage to the house is there? If there is we'll send somebody round, but it won't be until the end of the week I'm afraid.'

Mrs Williams put the phone down, Lorraine and Michael stayed until the end of the week, but it wasn't a happy house and in a way they were glad to be on their way. 'France again,' said her mother, 'you lucky pair, how long for this time Lorraine?' 'I don't know mum, looking at dad now I just want to get away from this place, it's horrible; it breaks people's hearts.' 'It's not the place love, it's just some of the people,' replied her mum. 'And if you don't mind Lorraine I don't think with your dad being the way he is, that it would be a good idea to see you to the station, he's still so depressed about what happened to his trees and all that, that I think he would feel even worse by saying goodbye to you both.' 'We understand mum, we'll say goodbye at the door.' And with the minimum of fuss Lorraine and Michael left for the station with the family waving goodbye from the garden gate.

Jimmy didn't bother with the trees again; the act of vandalism had taken the heart right out of it for him, and for some time he became withdrawn and unapproachable. 'Jimmy love, it's not doing you any good this moping around, why don't we go and get another couple of trees and you can start from scratch, it'll be so good to see you getting stuck in again. Don't let them beat you love, just stand up and show 'em they can't win.' 'I know you're right love, but I think my get-up-and-go's got up and gone, and anyway it's not the right time, when spring comes around I might feel different.'

Christmas came and went and things were getting a little better, but although Jimmy had got the gardening books out again, he was only reading. It was early May and Jimmy said to Janet, 'Don't cast a clout 'til May is out, that's what my mother used to say, but I'll tell you what girl, it's getting warmer by the minute, I suppose I shouldn't say so, but this global warming agrees with me. Let's have a walk down to the garden centre and see what we can pick up in the way of saplings.' 'And about time Jimmy Williams, I'll get our coats.' The garden centre had plenty to offer but Jimmy couldn't really see anything that seemed anywhere near as good has he had had before, and came away with a small pear tree. 'You don't have to rush,' said Janet, 'it's only early yet.'

Father's Day arrived and Janine and Freddy got their dad the usual stuff, a big block of Bourneville dark chocolate, DVD's of films that neither of them would be seen dead watching, and of course the obligatory cards that when opened, farted or screeched with maniacal laughter.

'Nowt from our Lorraine then,' said dad with a disappointed look on his face. 'They're not just round the corner Jimmy, maybe tomorrow,' said Janet.

Two days later a large parcel and a letter arrived within minutes of each other. Jimmy signed for the parcel, which looked a bit mysterious, and first opened the letter which had a French stamp on it, and which he hoped would be a card or some such thing from Lorraine. It was a card but not a comic one, in fact it was a bit on the sentimental side and made his eyes water a bit.

On the back of the card was a short note.

Dear dad hope things are well with you and all the clan, we're doing fine over here and tell mum that there's a wedding in the offing, I'll write to her all about it. It's a lovely apartment we've got here and it's right (get ready for this,) by the side of an orchard. We've got a view of the most beautiful golden delicious apples you could ever imagine, they melt in your mouth. Michael had a chat with the owner and he said that they love the sun and grow so well in a nice sheltered sunny location. Anyway to cut a long story short, there's a little tree on its way over to you from both of us with lots of love, and it goes without saying dad, but take care of it, and enjoy those golden apples of the sun.

Love you lot's Lorraine and Michael. XXXX

It might be a nice day

'Well dad what's the score, are you going to meet her? 'I don't really know, mate, it's been an awful long time you know?' Sally popped in with her two-penneth. 'How can you not know dad, she's your daughter for goodness sake; and (with a little excitement,) 'and my half sister as well. When was the last time you saw her?' 'I don't know, maybe thirty years or more, something like that,' said her dad. Jamie jumped in, his round red face nearly matching his ginger hair. 'And you've never thought about her in all that time, you just forgot she ever existed or what?'

'Listen lad I've had enough to do bringing you two kids up, it's not easy on the money that I've been on these last few years, and your mother always wants the best for us all, and none of that comes cheap. I've never had more than a few quid in my pocket after all the bills have been paid, and certainly not enough to fill the car up with two lots of petrol to go that distance. And time passes and it all becomes a distant memory, and my priorities changed; I had a new family to care for, and anyway we wouldn't even recognize each other. And goodness knows what we'd find to talk about.'

'John, when she was a baby she was your pride and joy; I know that, and it broke your heart…' 'OK Mary, I don't think the kids need to know the whole history…'But they do John, said his wife yet again, because all your past experiences make you the person you are. They need to know that you're not the kind of man who'd run out on his kids.'Turning to the children Mary began to explain the circumstances of how they came to have a half sister.' John disappeared outside for a smoke, pushing open the patio doors and leaving them open enough so that he could hear what was being said. His wife was one of the good ones and it had been the best thing he had ever done, marrying this sweet even- tempered girl, five foot two and eyes of blue and all that. He lit his cigarette, moved his angular body a little closer to the door opening and craned his neck to hear.

'The truth is, kids, that your Dad was married first to a woman he had been going out with for a long time, and he really should have known better than to marry her. He was too much in love with her to see things in a proper perspective. And when they got married she gave him the run around; they had the baby and he thought things might change. And they did, they changed for the worse. She cheated on him time and again until at last he couldn't take any more; it was destroying him inside. So he did the only thing he could and took the little one and got himself a small flat. It didn't take him long to realise that he couldn't make ends meet if he didn't work, this was forty years ago now and the state wasn't quite as good at throwing money about then, as it is today.

The outcome was that she had to go back to her mother and he only saw her on special occasions; birthdays, Christmas and the like, and in the thirty five years since we moved down here he's not seen her at all, and they lost contact completely until the letter came the other day; now regardless of what your dad says, I think you should at least know that much. So Jamie go and bring the old fool in from outside before he smokes himself to death.'

'I can hear ya, I might be an old fool but I'm not deaf you know.' 'Pardon?' said Mary. 'You heard' he said, coming across the room to put an arm round her, 'What would we do without this old girl.' he said. 'Never mind the old, go and put the kettle on and we'll make the decision between us, we're a family you know and I shouldn't have to tell you that.'

Five minutes later, John appeared at the kitchen door with four mugs of tea and a half eaten box of jammy dodgers. 'Dad, said Sally questioningly; do you love me as much as you loved her?' Well for a start 'her' has a name and her name is Joy; although looking back it might not have been the most fitting name to have given her, and to answer your question, Joy was three years old when her mother and I separated, but before that I had a beautiful time with my first born child. But Sally I've had a glorious twenty five years of knowing and loving you.'

Sally came over and gave her dad a big sloppy kiss. 'What's that for?' he said. 'That's just for being my dad' she said with a tear rolling down her cheek, 'and go and see Joy, please dad, after all the time she's taken to find you and eventually to write.' 'What do you think Jamie?' said his dad.'I think you're all going soft he said; get a bag packed; get on the train tomorrow; and go and see her, if you don't want to speak to her I'll phone her and tell her to expect you. Come on dad stand up for yourself; you're getting soft in your old age.'

Mary already had the railway timetables up on the internet. 'There's a train due from Old Road Station into Manchester at two thirty tomorrow, if Jamie phones now and lets Joy know you'll be there, you'll both have plenty of time to get yourselves sorted. And I'll phone in to work and tell them you've got a bad chest or something; you retire in six months anyway it's not as though they'll sack you is it?'

'I'm shaking like a leaf just thinking about it' said John, 'it's all so long ago now; wouldn't it be better just to write and go down and see her another time.' 'Johnny Barlow, I thought you had more courage than that, you've seen us all through thick and thin these last thirty years and now you're frightened of going to see your own flesh and blood; don't let her down,' and looking him straight in his eye, 'she wants to see her dad, don't take that away from her.'

John sniffed and coughed lightly, while rummaging in his pocket for his hankie, 'I think I've got a cold coming on love,' 'Yes well it's an early night for us all my lad, we don't want you missing that train do we?'

Sally was bouncing around like a two year old. 'Don't forget to take the camera dad, and get some nice pictures. In the one she sent with the letter she looks like you, so we need better than that, and make an attempt to keep it in focus, and most importantly don't cut her off at her shoulders.'

'I'm not David Bailey you know?' 'Dad' said Jamie, 'it's digital; it does it all for you, how anyone can make a mess of photos like you do, I don't know, and who the heck is David Bailey?' 'A bit before your time Jamie,' said his mother. 'Anyway,' Jamie said, 'I'm off out, if you're not still up when I get back, best of luck for tomorrow dad,' and muttered, 'I love you.' 'Listen who's talking about going soft,' said Sally, and ran off laughing. 'Thanks lad, I'll do my best.'

'John what say we watch that DVD we got at weekend and then have a cup of hot chocolate and an early night, it's my bet that you won't sleep much anyway but you can at least try,' and Mary went into the kitchen to where she'd left the film.

'Mary, do you think it will go alright?' 'John you've been shuffling about all night, try and get some sleep, you won't do yourself any favours if you let your daughter see her father looking like he's been dragged through a hedge backwards.

And everything's sure to be alright; she wants to see you just as much as you want to see her.' Mary turned and kissed him on the cheek. 'Don't worry love it'll be fine, now try and grab a couple of hours sleep at least."

The alarm shocked John out of a deep dream- filled sleep, for a moment or two he didn't know quite where he was. Then he remembered what the day had in store for him and butterflies made a home in his stomach. Mary was up already; cooking his breakfast and making him a flask and some sandwiches for the train journey.

'Now you know where to get off? She asked. 'Salford Station you said, I used to collect train numbers there when I was a kid, I never had the train spotting books like some of the others, but yeah I know all around that area.'

'John,' said Mary, it is possible, just a little bit, that maybe they've torn down a few old and built a few new, buildings there in the last fifty years, so it may not be exactly as you remember it, and we don't want you getting lost and missing the place altogether do we?' 'Get away with you woman, I'm not senile yet, it'll be an adventure, I'll be like Indiana Jones in that film we watched last night.' 'Oh for goodness sake' she said, and put his breakfast on the table.

'Mary, I still don't know how we're going to pay for this trip, I haven't any spare cash.' 'Don't worry about a thing love, I've paid for and reserved your ticket on line and here's a hundred pound in cash and I hope you both have a lovely day.'

'But…' 'Never mind how; it's all sorted, just you think about that girl of yours.' 'I've got my girl right here,' he said giving her a hug and a kiss in that order. 'Hmm tastes nice that bacon,

I might do some for myself,' she said, and just got out of the way of his hand reaching out to slap her backside.

At ten thirty the train pulled out of Old Street Station with a very nervous John on board the first carriage. Not like the old steam trains, he thought clickety clack and all that, a bit too slick, not the class of the old uns, still what were these days?

He'd got Joy's photo in his hand, it was true what Sally had said, she did look like him, the same nose and eyes, but her ears were not quite as prominent or maybe that was because of her hairstyle. Long blonde hair just like her mothers; he thought again about Ruth and the way it had all ended, and then instantly dismissed those old sad memories and thought anew about his wife of thirty years. She'd been and still was a good un; a real rock, he could rely on her for anything, she'd stabilised him through the years and put him back on the right track, they had a strong family and two lovely, loving kids.

A woman sitting nearby said. 'It's brightening up now it looks as if it might be a nice day after all, what was the forecast do you know?' 'I'm sorry' said John 'I didn't take much notice; I was a bit preoccupied.' And he told her what he had in front of him that day. 'Well I really hope all goes well for you and you get your daughter back, it must be so exciting for you. The next stop's mine.' she said, and with that she was gone.

She was right; it was exciting he thought as he wiped perspiration from his shirt collar; the butterflies were back with a vengeance; nerves on edge again. He looked at the photograph once more, just to remind himself of how lovely Joy had grown. He needed to keep the image in mind, he mustn't miss her as she stood there waiting for him. After all these years; He couldn't believe it, and he was a granddad as well, he'd teach the lad a thing or two if he got the chance. They'd have a real good time of it; but then maybe his other granddad wouldn't let him get a look in Maybe Joy might not want to see him again and it would all come to nothing. How foolish he was to think that it would be just the same after all these years.

He was sweating even more now and his chest hurt, Mary had always said he smoked too much. The train was approaching Salford Station now and he looked excitedly out of the window; and he saw her; long blonde hair, and taller than he had expected with a kiddie, also blond haired, and having lost the baby face, now starting with the looks of a fine young boy. They stood side by side; waiting in anticipation.

The urge to run to her and hold her as he had when she was a little baby, overcame him.

John had never had a heart attack before, and it was for sure he was never going to have another. He clutched at his chest his face distorted in pain, and then slumped back down into his seat, lifeless; and the train slowed and stopped and then continued on its way to the terminus passing on its way a young child waiting once more to see her dad, who would again throw her up to the moon and catch her as she came back down.

Travelling Light

It had been a long hard winter and now spring was in the air, time for a new start, or so Joe thought. He'd been at this game too long and now it was getting the better of him, he was just too old. Time was catching up with him, he was too long in the tooth, all those clichés, but they all made sense to him now. He'd being doing this since his early twenties and it was good money, not a lot of work to it, but you had to know what you were doing and reliability counted for all. Men could get killed in his line of work, and some he knew, had been.

He called in the club on his way home, he was always welcome there, and this was one of those places where at times offers of work came thick and fast, professionals like him were thin on the ground.

Tonight was a quiet night, not too many in, which suited him well. Apparently there had been a purge on somewhere and people were busy elsewhere. He had a few games of pool with a couple of the younger lads who were in, and came out even, so he was quite pleased about that. Experience overcame youth sometimes, and it was good for the soul especially at his time of life, and it lifted the brown study he was in. Joe went to the bar for another drink and sat ordered, then ate a bar meal of bangers and mash. It had been a long time since he had felt so relaxed, but he wondered how long it might last. Was it just the thought of getting out and starting afresh, and just be a fleeting thing, or would he feel this way when all had changed, hopefully for the better.

He'd been lucky all along, maybe his luck was about to turn bad, it was a thing he hadn't thought about in his youth, but now it was continually on his mind. There were nights when he laid awake thinking when the time might come when he wouldn't return home, and sometimes when he was called upon to work during the night, he thought about it during most of the day.

He was, he thought, with a wry twist of humour, just an ordinary Joe. He was of average height, average build, 'although he was putting a few extra pounds on these days,' he had no obvious distinguishing marks whatsoever that could set him apart from the average man in the street. It was this ordinariness that had kept him at the top of his game for so long. He had an ordinary family, two kids', one of each and a 'sometimes' caring wife. Like a lot of marriages, love had faded a long time ago but they got on well enough, if nothing else.

His work, as dangerous as it was, had been well paid enough to have given them a good life for a long time, financially speaking. The line of work he was in was his own affair and had been so throughout his life. There were certain aspects of it, that if were public domain would not be comfortable for him at all. There were times of course when he wondered if he would be missed if the worst were to happen He'd done his best throughout his married life to be a good husband and father and through it all he'd hoped he'd succeeded, but he didn't know and couldn't tell. He'd been born with this insecurity, and his job was the only thing he was certain of.

This was another part of the equation and one that he really didn't want to consider, but consider he had to. How would his and his family's life be affected by the change. What would happen if he couldn't find other employment, and had to struggle to make ends meet, his house was bought and paid for, but if he could find no alternative work how would the kids cope without him paying for their frequent holidays abroad and all the other extras that money had bought. Even though they were grown up, they still relied on him, much more so than they had any need to. They both had good jobs and were doing well, but worst of all how would his wife manage with him at home getting under her feet all and every day. It had seemed so easy on first thinking of it but now it was a bigger problem than he had ever envisaged.

A tap on the shoulder caused him to look round, 'Hi Joe'; it was an old friend of his from way back. 'How's it going Jack lad, long time no see.' 'It's not going well at all Joe, jobs are few and far between these days, I'm sorry I got out of the business now.' 'It's funny you should mention that Jack, I was thinking along the same lines myself, wondering whether to get out or not.'I'd think twice about it if I were you, it's a bad old world out there' said Jack, glancing at Joe's drink on the bar. 'Sorry mate I wasn't thinking, what will you have?' I'll have a small whiskey if that's okay,' 'You'll have a large one and say no more about it' said Joe. 'I don't see many old friends these days, it seems as if they've disappeared or are cluttering up the cemetery.' They sat at the bar and reminisced over old times, for an hour or so. Little did Jack know how much he had helped ease Joe's burden.

'Anyway Jack, I've got an early start tomorrow and it could be my last day, so take care,' and shoving a twenty pound note in Jacks top pocket, he said 'All the best' and went out through the doors and into the street and made his way home.

It was dark and quiet in the house as he put the key in the lock and opened the door. His wife would be out with her friends; Bingo, a few drinks, and jellied eels on the way home. She seemed to enjoy that more than any holiday they'd ever been on. He went straight to bed; he knew she wouldn't wake him knowing he had an early start the next day. He spent a fitful night's sleep and was out of bed in plenty of time, showered, shaved and suited, he pecked his still sleeping wife on the cheek and went out through the door.

His first job of the day was to pick up Mr Moran, and he was a stickler for punctuality, but Joe as reliable as ever turned up on the dot, then he made two other calls and five minutes later at six minutes past the hour Mr Moran said 'Second on the left here Joe' and Joe pulled in to the kerbside and stopped The three men with a holdall each, entered the building.

Joe got out of the car and moved to the rear and opened the boot, then moved leisurely back into the driver's seat, switching the ignition back on he sat there with the engine idling-just like a cat purring- Mr Moran always ensured his vehicles were in the best running order, for obvious reasons. In less than ten minutes the three men emerged from the building with bulging holdalls and walking swiftly to the car and threw them into the now open boot.

Joe floored the accelerator and with a squeal of tyres and burning rubber was on his way before any of the men could get in the car, the boot slamming shut with the impetus. Joe had made his mind up, this was his last day, and the rest of his life was his own. He'd been a getaway driver for robbers for the best part of thirty years, but this one was his. He'd ditch the car where he'd parked the second hand one he'd bought two days before, and he'd be on his way. He'd probably lie low up north for three or four weeks, grow some facial hair, get himself sorted and then book a flight to Rio. It would be good to start over.

Old Sal

The sound that pierced his ears and stopped him in his tracks had him rigid in shock and disbelief.

George had taken early retirement because of ill health, but after twelve months of sitting idly at home he had got himself a job as night watchman at a nearby clothing factory. He'd been employed there for nearly ten years and left on the advice of a friend, to 'get back into the world of the living' and to try his hand at labouring on a building site, the money was better, but he was not happy there, too much noise and madness, everyone pushing each other to get the job done. And in truth it was a bit too much like hard work at his time of life.

He missed the solitude of nights on his own walking up and down and around, the three floors of the factory that had once reverberated to the sounds of machinery fan belts, cogs and gear wheels racing against each other and the shouts and hubbub of the cotton mill to which this old building had years before leant itself, and as soon as he had got the chance he was back working there again.

The chap who had taken his place, one Tommy Reagan an old mate of Georges from way back, had phoned the owner, just a month after he had started there and mumbled down the phone that, 'something was not quite kosher here' in the early hours of one Tuesday morning, and saying that he was on his way home while he was still able. George attested to the fact, that it was at times quite eerie as he trod the old creaking wooden floorboards, with just his flash-light and the moon's glow shining through the windows to keep him company, but it didn't bother him in the least. The clothing consisted mostly of

Ladies attire, dresses, or frocks as he called them; skirts, coats, scarves, sweaters, trousers, evening wear, summer wear, winter wear and any other kind of wear that you could possibly imagine, that was if you had nothing better to do with your time, and at times there was a distinctive fragrance of lavender about the place, which was comforting to him as lavender had been a particular favourite of his wife.

The three floors were four deep on either side with racks and racks of each and every size, and each and every style, to suit old or young and small or large, and sewing machines in a line down the middle.

There had been some debating amongst the girls who worked there during the day whether or not it had been 'Old Sal' who had scared Tommy away, but he hadn't said, and didn't know and uttered nothing other than, 'something's not quite kosher there.'

'Old Sal' as legend had it, was the spirit of an old dear who walked about in ragged clothing, bewailing the fact that all these clothes were there doing nothing while so many of her kind were without, and freezing to death in the process. There were others who said that she was the ghost of an old mill worker looking for her long dead son who had died at the mill, caught and mangled up in the machinery whilst scavenging for cotton. The old lady it seemed was a precursor to the demise or unhappiness of someone close to the observer, but it was now a month or so after Tommy's experience and although his son Jimmy had been involved in a slight bump in his car, all was well, so as George said, 'It was just a coincidence that's all.' George had heard all these rumours countless times, but he himself had seen nothing of any ghost in the years he had been there, although there were times when cats had got in once or twice and he had heard them howling, and occasionally had caught a glimpse of something or somebody out of the corner of his eye, but on investigation had decided on it being a trick of the light. Other noises he attributed to the many mice scuttling around the building, fighting over the leftovers of the girls' lunches from during the day.

George had been on his own now, twelve years coming up to this April 5th, when his dear wife Emily had passed away quite suddenly, leaving lots of things unsaid and undone between them. He'd wandered around rudderless for a long while and being childless he had descended into his own private world.

He had taken early retirement as he just couldn't pull himself together. It took him an age to come to terms with his loss and it was soon after, that he had got this job back, he'd got used to his own company and he walked the floors every night with his memories. He remembered her soft silky hair and the slightness of her body, her tinkling laugh and the blush that came to her cheeks, as before going out he would look at her and tell her how beautiful she looked, 'Get away' she'd say 'anyone would think I was a girl' 'You are to me' he'd say and peck her on her cheek, and she'd blush again. It seemed a different lifetime now, as if it had been only a dream. He missed her so very much.

Every six weeks or so he would have to work two or three hours assisting the girls during the day, as the stock was moved out to retail outlets, and some more materials would be delivered from the manufacturers. It was during one of these spells that he trapped his leg between the trolley he was unloading from the container lorry, and the barrier post at the warehouse goods entrance. He at first thought he'd crushed his foot and couldn't bear to look down at what he thought would be his shattered ankle. Jenny the first aider on the factory floor there, divested him of his shoe and sock and applied a cold poultice, sat him down and said 'It doesn't feel like there are any bones broken George, but it seems a bit swollen, perhaps a night off might be in order.' 'I'll be okay' George assured her 'a bit of kip and I'll be fine.'

She fitted him out with an elastic ankle bandage, a couple of strong painkillers, and a half a box more just in case he couldn't get to the chemist before they closed, and he had a cup of tea, then re- assuring the boss that he would be back later, made his way home for a couple of hours sleep before the start of his night shift.

The girls were blaming 'Old Sal' again but as George said 'he hadn't had the pleasure.'

It was eight pm when he unlocked the factory gate and let himself in, it was a bright moonlit night and he made his way to the canteen for a quick cuppa before starting the first round of the night, his foot was aching somewhat but it didn't seem too bad once he was mobile It was when he was on the top floor, halfway round his third tour of duty at about eleven thirty, that he heard the noise; it seemed to be coming from the floor below; a low sobbing sound accompanied by a high pitched wailing. He at first stood there rooted to the spot, then assumed it was probably cats again; they would get in through the back door when the girls were on their way off home, they'd been after the mice that had been after the food scraps the girls had left, who had left the door open for the cats to get in and so it went on. He'd mentioned it to the girls on previous occasions and they had kept a look-out and he had had no trouble for a good while.

Still he thought it best to investigate and made his way to the stairs and down to the next floor. He pushed open the doors to the middle floor, and the shambling wreck of a person that stood before him illuminated in the moonlight, took his breath away; an old woman grey and gaunt, dressed in filthy rags, sobbing and wailing, wringing her hands and moaning 'Where is my boy, my dear only boy, where is he; why can I not find him in this God forsaken place, full of rich clothing for the well-to-do while we scrimp and starve, Oh where oh where is my precious boy?'

George's mouth opened but no sound came out and he turned and fled down the stairs knocking his uninjured ankle in the process, stumbling down two or three stairs until his feet went from beneath him, and trying to regain his balance and failing, proceeded to fall head-first; tumbling head over heels down the full flight, to lie in a crumpled heap at the bottom, and before he passed over his senses were filled with the most beautiful fragrance of lavender, and the softly spoken words of his dear wife Emily 'I've tried to keep her away George but this time she was too strong for me, but we'll be together now, I've been waiting such a long time.

The Battle for the Kingdoms Series

Book One: Bones lay Bleaching

Chapter One: (abridged excerpt)

1. What lies before us

The avian creature's wings spread wide, across and over its victim's still writhing body and its curved razor edged beak continued to feast upon its prey. Held down by its powerful talons, its constantly moving head and deep black eyes searching for anything that might attempt to snatch this meal from it's grasp, the winged assassin gorged; there was no escape for its victim, until minutes later the screams and cries of the Moraki sentry were stilled; and all that could be heard was the tearing of flesh as the Raakon devoured its prey...

High Marshal Josefus; he of Human and leonine descent raised himself from his seat and faced the council, he was an old soldjer who had fought at Orram with Morogar Ra; he had been a Colonel then and had been badly injured, his right eye put out by the glancing blow of a Galtan battle axe thrown by a soldjer already on his way to join his forefathers in the next world, and a scar from the crown of his head down to his throat told the tale of how close he had come to following his attacker to realms unknown. All around him were seated the supreme leaders of Morak.

His one good eye looked from one to the other first alighting on his ruler. Ragnan Ra was the closest to a complete non- animal specimen; the God line, the rest were deviants in one way or another. Josefus himself had more animal characteristics lying just beneath the surface; far back in time his ancestors had been more animal than Human. Others were more or less in varying degrees, as opposed to the opposite with the Galtans, who were by far the nearer to animal. He stood proud and dominant and a true picture of a warrior in his gleaming chain mail with his mighty broadsword at his side and his visored helmet on the great meeting table in front of him. He was well respected as head of all Morak's forces, and even before he had attained that status his opinion had been sought on many occasions.

He pushed aside his lion's mane and addressed the forum; "As you know" he said quietly to the assembled dignitaries. "In the years before the beginning of this great war when all Moraki and Galtans lived and traded peacefully together under the reign of Agram Ra, unions were made between us that produced the Xubile who were of smaller number and were virtually eradicated by the Galtans because they had sided with us at the outbreak of the hostilities between our nations. The survivors of their kind had joined others of their kin and made exodus to and have been living in, the wilderness in the south of Galta ever since those terrible times. It seems to me that since then they will have grown greatly in numbers and may well be persuaded to join us if only to avenge the wrong done to them and their kind, those many years ago."

"That is all very well" said Dargan the leader of the southern Partment of the country which had included the townlet of Kazna that now lay in ashes. He was of bovine descent, with all the wrong traits of the lineage, Josefus had been wary of him ever since he, Josefus, had been given the title High Marshal; the feeling of bitter envy from Dargan every time he came within sight of Josefus was plain for most to see.

"But," continued Dargan laughing derisively, "You would have to pass deep into the country of the Galtans therefore risking the lives of many more of our troops to get to them, and we have in no way assisted them in their troubles. What makes you think that they would even consider joining us?"

Josefus, with his mane now bristling and his fangs gnashing, turned to Dargan, claws beginning now to extend in smouldering anger. He would not bear scorn from this suspected quisling."I repeat what I said before partment leader, vengeance can be a very powerful ally," snarled Josefus, rising to his feet again. He was angry now and when he was angry his visage took on the more animal in him; there were some Moraki and Galtan, at times of extreme stress or emotion who would metamorphose into the part of their character best designed to deal with the situation, and Josefus leant a little too much to his animal instincts, which unfortunate as it was at times, made him the leader that he had become.

The next day dawned with its orange glow and a greyness in the sky mixed with vast areas of rainbow effect whorls that forecast the ice showers which could kill men and beast if caught out in the open. "General Athol we will strike out for the ancient city of Aacah, the trees here about us are neither large enough nor strong enough and will hold no protection from this weather. I have seen the downfall of this ice, slice trees like these to pieces. Aacah is but five miles away and we can take shelter there until the storm subsides," Josefus had been in ice storms before, on a foray into the unknowns, but never this far south; to him the weather was becoming more unpredictable as the years went by. The phantas were quickly mounted without their chain mail, and supply waggons and troopers fled before the storm.

Aacah was the Moraki name for this once great city of which the most part had been buried over the passage of time. There were many things there which had no meaning to anyone alive, except that which had been passed down in legend and myth. Most had been left to the mercy of the natural environment and assumed the status of a mystery that would never be solved.

The city lay crumpled; as a misshapen tumble of tents after a whirlwind had passed through a camp; twisted metal rods of differing thicknesses stuck out at all angles from blocks of material that no axe could break, and no-one yet in these times could replicate. The answers to who had, and how this, city had been built lay in the mists of time and myth. There were many buildings in the vicinity which had been buried in the sands of time but the most accessible was the one in which they now sheltered, with the manscript of long ago, *A.A.C.A.H* emblazoned at which was now Moraki height; the Centyears of long past had named the city with that one word.

The Declon passed into this great structure by means of a massive breach in the wall, inside of which there was a huge hall. The men settled themselves down for what could be a long wait. After some time of the soldjers standing idle, Athol who was not of that disposition, enquired of Josefus. "While the storm is abroad High Marshal might it be beneficial to us that I may take a party to explore deeper into the recesses of this place; there may be something here that could be to our advantage?" "Take who you may General but remember that time is of the essence here and though these storms may last for days, the moment it has abated we must be on our way. This is not a trip for pleasure, Athol." "As you say Sir, I will take but three others, each one with a taper, and be back before the tapers have extinguished."

Then Athol turned toward the troop. "Sarjent Golan, troopers Datan and Atlan fall in behind me in single file, Major Ranra you are in temporary command of 1st Declon under High Marshal Josefus," "Yes Sir," Ranra replied, now standing from his previously seated position, with a salute to his superior officer.

The three then made their way to the head of the stepway, through the debris of centuries, then down into the depths of the building the taper lighting their way. They had but gone down three flights of steps when they found that the way was blocked.

"This would seem to be as far as we are able to go," said Athol; frustrated. Golan stepped forward and took hold of the lighted taper and thrust it in front of him."General, there appears to be a way to the side, we require another taper Sir to see any further; a cavern of sorts it seems to be." Trooper Datan hastened his slim frame forward to reach Golan's side, an extra light held before him.

"By the great God Yaway," he said and stepped back in alarm, "there is no ground before us Sir, but a great black abyss to which I see no bottom."

Read the full length novel **Bones lay Bleaching**, *book in the* **Battle for the Kingdoms** *series, by* **Roy Bolland**, *available soon on Amazon*

In a post-apocalyptic world, Earth is ravaged by an asteroid collision and nuclear contamination, leading to a dark and chaotic existence. The surviving population consists of mutated hybrids from various species.

Amidst the turmoil, Anakk Ra, ruler of Galta, initiates a war with neighbouring Morak, aiming to forcefully unite the kingdoms on the anniversary of a fragile truce.

High Marshal Josefus, a hybrid leonine creature and second-in-command to Morak's ruler, Ragnan Ra embarks on a dangerous mission to seek an alliance with the Xubile, from the Wasteland crucial for the defense of their countries. Joined by Modda, a deserter from Anakk Ra's forces, they devise a daring plan in the Xubile capital, uniting against their common enemy. With time running out, they must overcome treachery and obstacles to ensure the survival of their people and shape a new future in this forever-changed world.

About the Author.

I was born and bred at Irlams o' th' Height in that great City of Salford, near Manchester and first educated at St John's Infants school, just around the corner from the house where I was born. In between 'our street' and the next was a bowling green, a Library and a theatre, and three parks within walking distance, one of them with a museum, what a childhood filled with amazing memories.

I later attended Halton Bank Secondary Modern, with more memories of mostly great kids and knowledgeable, willing to impart teachers. I was rubbish at Maths and my best subject was what they then (in the 1950's) called 'Composition' I got really good marks and thoroughly enjoyed the writing of stories. This is the first time I have attempted to have anything published in book form and although I have lived in a lovely coastal area in North Wales for the most part of my life now, I'm still a 'Salford Lad' at heart. I've only got to open my mouth for anyone to know that.

Roy Bolland

Bones Lay Bleaching

Book One of The Battle for the Kingdoms

Roy Bolland

Printed in Great Britain
by Amazon

28871060R00050